GARFIELD

AND THE BEAST IN THE BASEMENT

About Garfield's Creator

Jim Davis is the award-winning creator of Garfield. He is the only author to have seven books appear simultaneously on the *New York Times* best-seller list.

Jim lives in Indiana. His hobbies include golf, fishing, and eating jelly doughnuts. An active environmentalist, Jim dreams of the day when there will be a cure for dog breath.

About the Author

Jim Kraft was a classics major at Kenyon College. Finding the market for Roman historians to be a tad depressed, he naturally turned to greeting card writing. Eventually he started writing for Garfield. He is the author of more than 60 children's books and several really snappy postcards.

Mr. Kraft lives in Carmel, Indiana, with his wife, two sons, and six basketballs.

About the Illustrator

Mike Fentz attended Herron School of Art in Indianapolis. After spending ten years crisscrossing the country as a caricaturist, Mike joined Paws, Inc. (the Garfield company), where he works as an artist, designing and illustrating children's books.

Mike lives in Muncie, Indiana, with his wife and two daughters. An avid runner, he hopes to compete in the Boston Marathon before he develops cataracts on his knees.

GARFIELD
AND THE
BEAST
IN THE
BASEMENT

Created by JIM DAVIS

Written by Jim Kraft

**Designed and Illustrated
by Mike Fentz**

The basement was damp and dusty. Most of all, it was dark. There were only two windows, both of them dirty. One window had a large hole that was covered by a piece of cardboard. Even on a sunny day it was gloomy in the basement. At night it was especially spooky.

And now it was midnight.

Two mice scurried across the basement floor.

"Find anything, Herb?" one mouse called to his brother.

"Not a crumb, Zeke," Herb replied.

"Try the laundry basket," Zeke suggested. "The cat sometimes puts mashed potatoes in the big guy's pant's pockets. If you find anything, give a squeak."

While Herb tried the laundry, Zeke scampered off to check a small hole in the kitchen floor. Sometimes crumbs fell through that hole.

Suddenly Zeke heard a heavy thumping on the floor above. It sounded like a hippopotamus. So it had to be the cat. *Going for his midnight snack,* thought Zeke.

The cat was fat and orange. He wasn't much of a mouser. In fact, he wasn't much of a *mover.* As long as Zeke and Herb stayed out of the cat's way, he left them alone.

Zeke took the shortcut under the workbench . . . and ran right through a spider's web. *Ugh!* thought Zeke, pulling the sticky strands from his whiskers. *Those spiders are always putting up new webs without telling anyone. I hate living with them. They're too sneaky.*

At that moment Zeke heard a loud squeak. He ducked back under the workbench.

The spider was already repairing her web. "Clumsy!" the spider hissed as the mouse passed by.

"Eat a bug," muttered Zeke.

He found his brother sitting in the laundry basket.

"Herb," said Zeke, "you're eating a dirty sock."

"The big guy spilled pizza sauce on them," answered Herb with his mouth full. "They're not bad. Do you want one?" He scooped up the matching

sock and held it out to his brother.

Zeke sighed. "I can't take it anymore, Herb. We're living in a dusty basement. We're surrounded by spiders. We're eating dirty socks for dinner. Doesn't it bother you?"

Herb nodded thoughtfully. "You're right, Zeke. Are you going to eat this sock? Because if you're sure you don't want it . . ."

"Be my guest," said Zeke. "But I'm telling you, Herb. Someday—"

Suddenly Zeke froze. He cocked his head. His nose twitched.

"What is it?" Herb whispered.

Zeke stuffed a smelly sock in his brother's jaws. Slowly he raised his head over the edge of the basket.

The basement was full of dark, scary shapes. But one particular shape caught Zeke's attention. It had eyes.

Lots of them. They were looking at Zeke. And they were moving toward him.

Zeke grabbed his brother by the arm. "Run, Herb!" he cried. "Run for your life!"

Jon's startled cry lifted Garfield off the seat of the easy chair.

"Wha . . . What is it?" asked Garfield, clinging to the arm of the chair. "Is the house on fire? Are the aliens invading? Did I miss lunch?"

Jon Arbuckle rushed into the room. "Garfield," he said, "I just saw two mice in our kitchen."

Garfield rolled his eyes and sank back into the chair. "Is that all? I thought maybe the refrigerator had died. If you don't mind, I'm trying to watch *How Dumb Is Your Dog?*"

Jon put his hands on his hips. "Did you hear me, Garfield? I saw two mice in the kitchen."

"Really, Jon? Well, I saw three cockroaches in the bathroom. So I win."

Jon stepped in front of Garfield, blocking the fat cat's view of the TV.

"Hey! Hey!" Garfield complained. "They were just about to show a dog with his head stuck in a jar of peanut butter."

"Garfield, what are you going to do about the mice?" asked Jon.

"Do . . . ?" Garfield replied with amazement. "Why should I do anything? Let the mice eat some of your cooking. That will get rid of them."

"We all have certain duties here," Jon said sternly. "My duty is to make a good home for you and Odie. Odie's duty is to be a watchdog."

"And make a good home for fleas," Garfield added.

"And your duty is to keep mice out of our house."

"Sorry, I'm not into mice," said Garfield.

"I expect you to do your duty." Jon wagged a finger at his pet. "But I see you need a little push. So I'm putting you on a strict diet, starting right now. You'll stay on a diet until those mice are gone."

Garfield gasped. "A diet? I can't go on a diet! I have a growing tummy to feed!"

"Happy hunting, Garfield." Jon turned and walked out of the room.

"You'll never get away with this!" the fat cat cried. "I'll call my lawyer! I'll shred your underwear! I'll . . . I'll . . . I'll have to catch a mouse?"

Garfield slumped down in his chair. "Mice," he muttered. "Can't live with 'em, can't eat 'em. Yuck."

All that afternoon Garfield hoped that Jon would forget about his threat. But when dinnertime came around, it was clear that Jon had *not* forgotten.

Garfield frowned at his plate of lettuce, cottage cheese, and carrot sticks. "I can't eat this," he moaned. "My taste buds will die of boredom."

"Dig in, Garfield," Jon said. "That cottage cheese can be very filling."

"You're right," Garfield replied. "I think I'll use some to fill up your bunny slippers."

Clearly, if he was going to save

his stomach, he would have to do something about the mice.

"Okay, Odie," Garfield said to his friend that evening. "Let's sniff out those mice. Let's get on their trail. Let's go!"

Odie just stared at Garfield.

Garfield sighed and rolled his eyes. "You don't have any idea what I'm talking about, do you?"

Odie shrugged, sticking out his soggy tongue.

"Obviously you don't come from a long line of hunters," Garfield said. "More like a long stream of slobberers."

With Odie tagging along, Garfield searched for the mice. He didn't find them in the kitchen, or in Jon's closet, or behind Jon's dresser, or under Jon's bed. There were no mice creeping around the bathroom.

Garfield was going to check the

basement next, but Odie refused.

"What's the matter, you big scaredy-dog?" Garfield asked. "Afraid to go down in the spooky old basement?"

Odie gave a low growl and backed away.

"I'll bet there's a big dog-eating monster under the basement steps," Garfield teased.

Odie growled some more.

"I don't know why you're worried," Garfield told him. "No monster could ever stand up to your dog breath."

Garfield gazed down the steps. It was very dark at the bottom.

"No monsters down there," he decided. "Just spiders. Lots and lots of spiders. With their tiny spider legs and big spider fangs."

A trickle of terror ran down Garfield's spine.

"Odie, I don't want to shame you by going down there alone," Garfield said. Quickly he closed the door. "So let's forget the basement. If the mice are down there, then that's where they belong, right?"

Odie nodded eagerly.

"Our work here is done," Garfield decided. "Although we did forget to check for mice in the refrigerator."

But Garfield had barely opened the refrigerator door when Jon rushed in and slammed it shut.

"Oh, no, you don't, Garfield!" he barked. "I told you: You're on a diet until you get rid of those mice."

"But I did get rid of the mice," Garfield replied. "This house is one hundred percent rodent-free. I swear it on a stack of cookbooks!"

"I'm going to put out some cheese

tonight," Jon said. "If it hasn't been touched by morning, I'll know the mice are gone, and you can have pancakes as a reward. But no food until then."

"Well, come on, Odie," Garfield grumbled. "We might as well go to bed. Maybe I can dream up some lasagna."

Garfield threw himself down on his bed and pulled up the blanket.

"Hey!" cried a squeaky voice. "Quit hogging the covers!"

To Garfield's surprise, two mice crawled out from beneath his blanket.

"Mice!" said Garfield crossly. "I have mice in my bed. That does it. I'm definitely going to get a cat."

"Uh, Zeke?" Herb turned to his brother. "I thought *he* was a cat."

"I *am* a cat, you little cheese-eater," Garfield snarled. "But I'm more the lazy, overeating, let-the-servants-take-care-of-me kind of cat. What I need is a mouse-munching kind of cat."

"Why?" asked Zeke. "What did we ever do to you?"

"You broke the rules, mouse," Garfield explained. "You should have stayed down in the basement and out of the kitchen. You made me look bad in front of my owner. Now, thanks to you, I'm on a diet. I'll bet I've lost ten pounds already."

"Well, you could stand to lose a few more," squeaked Herb.

Garfield glared at the mouse. "How would you like a ride in the garbage disposal?"

"Listen, cat," Zeke cut in. "We're sorry if we got you into trouble, but we're not going back in that basement. We're tired of eating crumbs down there. We want to eat crumbs up here. We want to scamper on carpet. We want

to chew on *clean* socks for a change. We want a better life. We want *your* life."

"Sorry," said Garfield. "I'm using my life right now. You know the rules. Pampered cats live upstairs. Pesky mice live downstairs. So crawl back to the basement and no one gets hurt."

"But we can't go back down there," Herb protested.

"Why not?" Garfield asked.

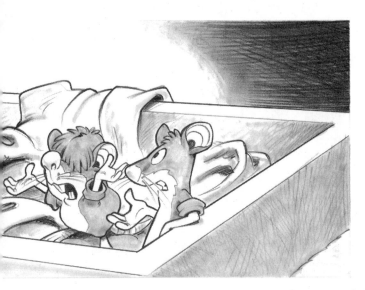

Herb's face turned as white as his round tummy. "Because . . . the *beast* is down there."

"What *beast*?" said Garfield.

"The beast in the basement," Zeke told him. "We saw it last night. It tried to eat us."

"But it didn't," Herb added. "It's big. Great big. Huge."

"It's pretty big," agreed Zeke.

"With about fifty eyes," gasped Herb.

"More like seven or eight," Zeke corrected.

Garfield looked from one mouse to the other. "Nice try," he said. "But even Odie wouldn't fall for that story."

"But it's true!" the mice argued.

"Right," Garfield replied. "When you're back in the basement, be sure to get the beast's autograph for me. Now, beat it."

"We can't!" said Herb.

"We won't!" Zeke insisted.

Garfield sighed. "You know, I don't want to eat you mice"—he bared a single claw—"but maybe I could use you as a scratching post."

"Run, Herb! Run for your life!" cried Zeke.

"Boy, am I getting tired of hearing that," muttered Herb.

Garfield was much too slow to catch the mice. But the effort made him even more tired than usual. He dragged himself back to bed, where he quickly fell asleep.

Later that night, when the whole house was dark, Garfield heard an unusual noise.

"Odie, you're barking in your sleep again," Garfield mumbled. "Cut it out." He rolled over and dozed off again.

He had a strange dream. He dreamed he was lying in the sink.

Water was dripping on his nose. Drip, drip, drip. Garfield tried and tried, but he could not move his head away from the drip. Finally, it woke him up.

Odie was standing over him, with his tongue hanging out.

"Ack!" Garfield complained. "What a way to wake up! Get out of here, you leaky pup!"

"Shhh!" said Odie. He pointed. A noise was coming from the kitchen.

Garfield got out of bed. "Probably

30

those pesky mice again," he whispered to Odie. "Let's give them a good scare."

The two pets tiptoed to the kitchen. When they peeked around the doorway, they heard a grunt of alarm, then the clatter of feet on the tile floor. It was too dark to see very much. But Garfield and Odie saw *something*. It was a mysterious black shape, and it disappeared down the basement stairs.

Garfield and Odie looked at each other. "Did you sort of see what I sort of saw?" Garfield asked.

Odie gulped and nodded.

"That was not a mouse."

Odie shook his head.

"That was much too big to be a mouse. So what was it?"

Odie shrugged.

"Well, we know one thing for sure. The mice were right: There *is* a beast in our basement."

Garfield and Odie looked fearfully at the basement door. Then they raced into the bedroom and dove under the covers with Jon.

Neither pet slept any more that night.

"Aha!" cried Jon the next morning when he saw the empty plate in the kitchen. "The cheese is gone. That means the mice are still here. And you, Garfield, are still on a diet."

"Jon, I've been trying to tell you," Garfield replied. "We have a bigger problem than mice. Much bigger. And scarier."

"I have to go out today," Jon went on. "I hope you get rid of those mice while I'm gone. If you don't, I'll have to buy some mousetraps."

"We don't need mousetraps!" said Garfield. "We need the marines!"

Later that day Garfield and Odie found the mice hiding under the kitchen sink.

"I owe you two crumb-collectors an apology," Garfield said. "You were right. There really *is* a beast in the basement."

"Told you so," Herb replied.

"Last night it paid a visit to the kitchen," Garfield revealed.

"We know. We heard it," Zeke told him. "Did you get a good look at it?"

Garfield shook his head. "It was too dark. But it looked pretty big."

"It's enormous," Herb agreed, wide-eyed. "It's green. It has three horns and six-inch fangs and terrible claws that will slice you into confetti. Eeeeeek!"

Herb fainted.

"Does the beast really look like that?" asked Garfield.

"You'll have to excuse Herb," Zeke said. "He has too much imagination."

"And not enough brains," Garfield snapped.

Zeke helped Herb get back on his feet.

"Sorry," said Herb, holding his head. "I guess I'm a little weak from lack of food."

"Aren't we all," Garfield grumbled.

"We've hardly touched a crumb for the last two days," said Zeke. "I'm so hungry I could eat a dirty sock. Is there anything in the refrigerator?"

"I think there's some of Jon's homemade meat loaf," Garfield replied.

"How is it?" Zeke asked.

"It tastes like dirty socks."

"Let's eat!" said Herb.

Before going to sleep that night, Jon set out another plate of cheese. Then he put on his pajamas, brushed his teeth, and pushed Garfield and Odie out of his bed.

"I hope the beast eats him first," growled Garfield, stomping off.

The fat cat flopped onto his bed and pulled the blanket around his head. Odie watched him with sad eyes. He whimpered softly.

"Oh, all right," said Garfield. "You can sleep with me tonight."

A few minutes later Zeke and

Herb tapped on Garfield's bed. "Room for two more?" Zeke asked.

"This is not a hotel," said Garfield.

"Please?" begged the mice.

"Well, okay." Garfield gave in. "But don't touch my teddy bear."

The four animals pressed close to one another. Wide awake, they watched and listened for the beast.

"I can't stand this," Garfield said at last. "We can't lie here waiting for that monster. I have a plan."

"What kind of plan?" asked Zeke.

"A brilliant kind of plan," Garfield replied. "I call it . . . Plan A."

Garfield led the others into the kitchen. "We'll set a trap for this beast," he said. "Here's what we'll do."

While the mice spread butter all over the kitchen floor, Garfield and

Odie peeled eight bananas. They ate the bananas and dropped the peels on the floor. Then Garfield set a stack of pots and pans on top of the refrigerator, very close to the edge.

"First, the beast will slip on the banana peels," explained Garfield. "Then he'll slide across the buttered floor and slam into the refrigerator. This will cause the pots to crash down on his head. While he's stunned, we can rush in and tie him up."

Everyone agreed it was a good plan. They all squeezed back into Garfield's bed. There they waited.

And waited.

And waited.

Long after midnight, when everyone was sound asleep, there was a loud CRASH! Garfield, Odie, and the mice spilled out of bed.

"We got him!" cried Garfield. "We

bagged the beast!" They ran to the kitchen. Odie turned on the light.

A dazed Jon Arbuckle lay flat on his back, with pots and pans all around him. A soup pot was stuck on his head.

"Owww!" groaned Jon. "What happened? I just wanted a snack."

"That's not the great big beast," said Herb.

"You're right," agreed Garfield. "That's a great big bonehead."

Suddenly Odie began to bark. He pointed to the kitchen table.

"Look!" gasped Garfield.

Once again, the cheese was gone.

8

"The beast didn't fall for our trap," said Garfield the next morning. "So it's time to try Plan C."

"What happened to Plan B?" asked Zeke.

"Plan B is where a meteor crashes into the basement and conks the beast on the head," Garfield told him. "I don't think we can count on that. What we need to do is . . ." Garfield paused. Odie and the mice leaned toward him. ". . . go down to the basement and face the beast."

Odie's ears stood straight up in

the air. With a "yip!" he ran into Jon's bedroom and dove under the bed.

Garfield shook his head. "What a weenie. If they had a magazine for cowards, Odie would be on the cover every month. Well, that still leaves three of us."

"May I say something?" asked Herb.

"Of course," said Garfield.

"Move over, dog!" Herb cried. He raced after Odie.

Garfield looked at Zeke. "And you?"

"Count me in," said Zeke. "You know, cat, I didn't know you were so brave."

"Yeah, well . . . thanks," mumbled Garfield. "I'm either really brave or really nuts. The truth is, I'm just sick and tired of dieting. And I'm tired of

losing sleep. I want to settle this beast thing, one way or another."

"So do I," Zeke agreed.

Garfield went to the hall closet. He came back with Jon's tennis racket grasped firmly in his paw.

"What's that for?" asked Zeke.

"For beast bashing, what else?"

Moments later Garfield and Zeke stood at the top of the basement stairs. Garfield flicked the light switch. A dim light came on at the bottom of the stairs.

"It doesn't look so spooky if you don't think about it," said Garfield.

"Or look at it," added Zeke.

"It's awfully quiet down there. Do you think the beast is home?"

"Where would he go?" Zeke asked. "To the movies?"

"Hey, beast!" Garfield called down the stairs. "Are you there?"

Silence.

Garfield tried again. "A nice beast like you shouldn't be living in a dusty basement like this!"

"It's not even fit for a mouse," Zeke chimed in.

"You should move someplace nicer! Like the beach! You could be the beast of the beach!"

There was no reply from the dark basement.

"I guess we're going to have to do this the hard way," said Garfield. "Ready, mouse?"

"Ready, cat."

Garfield and Zeke started slowly down the stairs.

By the time they reached the last step, both Garfield and Zeke were sweating.

The two beast-hunters glanced around the basement. There were lots of dark pockets where anything might be hiding. Piles of junk and stacks of boxes were everywhere.

"What a mess," said Garfield.

"But we mice call it home," Zeke replied sarcastically.

Garfield was looking at a cobweb-covered hulk resting on Jon's workbench. "I remember that toaster. It used to

shoot toast into the air. Then Jon fixed it. After that it just shot flames into the air."

Zeke tugged on Garfield's paw. "Over there," he whispered. "That's where I saw the beast."

Zeke was pointing to a shadowy corner of the basement. At the edge of

the shadows stood a table. It was covered with a large piece of canvas that draped to the floor. Old newspapers and empty coffee cans were stacked on top of the canvas.

Garfield's knees started shaking. "On second thought," he said very slowly, "maybe we should turn around, go back upstairs, and move to another continent. What do you say?"

"We've come this far," Zeke urged. "Let's take a look."

Cat and mouse crept across the

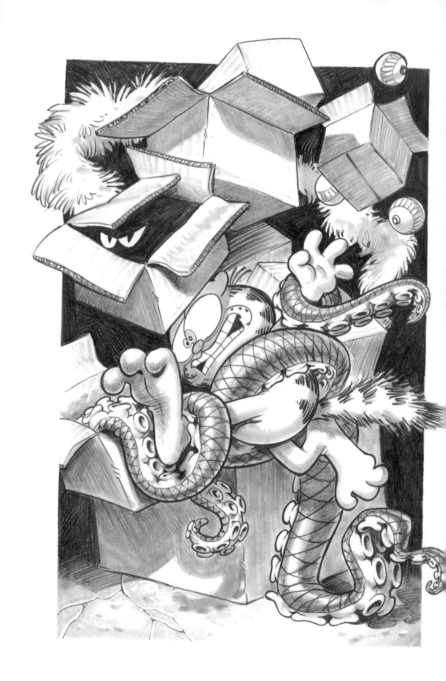

floor until they reached a tall stack of boxes beside the table. Garfield leaned against the cartons, his heart banging like a coconut in a clothes dryer.

A small box toppled off the stack and smacked onto the floor.

"The beast!" cried Garfield. In a panic he crashed straight into the other boxes. They fell all around him.

"Mouse! It's got me!" Garfield screamed. "Heeeelp!"

Garfield felt furry monster arms coiling around his body! Deadly fangs began digging into his neck!

"So long," groaned Garfield. "Say good-bye to the refrigerator for me."

"Maybe I should say 'happy holidays,'" Zeke suggested.

Garfield stopped struggling. He opened his eyes and looked down.

"Christmas lights?" he asked.

Strands of Christmas lights had fallen out of the boxes and landed on Garfield. Now they were wound in a tangled knot around his large body. His desperate efforts to escape had only pulled the knot tighter.

"That's some ferocious beast," said Zeke with a smile.

"Hey!" Garfield scowled. "These

things can be very dangerous. Why, uh, in the wild, a pack of untamed Christmas lights can bring down a full-grown water buffalo. It's true. I saw it on TV."

Zeke rolled his eyes. Then he helped the cat get free.

"These lights won't mess with *me* again," Garfield said, kicking at the tangled heap of wires. "I kicked their bulbs. I—"

Zeke threw up his hand to silence Garfield. He snapped his tiny head from side to side.

"You heard something?" Garfield asked quietly.

The mouse nodded.

"Where?"

Zeke pointed under the table.

"What should we do?" Garfield said.

But before the cat and mouse could decide, two things happened.

First, the basement was plunged into darkness.

"AAAAAAH!" screamed Garfield and Zeke.

"Okay, okay," gasped Garfield, panting with fear. "So the light went out. No problem. Cats can see in the dark—which means I'll get a real good look at the beast right before he tears us to pieces!"

"I don't like this, cat," squeaked Zeke. He clung tightly to Garfield's knee.

"We'll get out of here," said Garfield in a shaky voice. "We'll turn around and go back up the steps. We can still see the way. The door is still open. We don't need to panic."

Then the basement door slammed shut.

Stunned, Garfield and Zeke stood like statues in the darkness. For a long moment they were silent. Finally, in a thin whisper, Zeke said, "Uh, cat? What happens now?"

"It's very simple," Garfield replied. "We do a little number that I like to call . . . PANIC TIME!"

10

Blinded by fear, the frantic fat cat rumbled through the darkness like a runaway bowling ball. He ran over boxes. He crashed into walls. He fell over paint cans. He slammed into poles. He was bruised and battered, but he was so afraid he didn't even feel the bumps. Several times he was certain the beast

had grabbed him. Each time he fought his way free. Finally, after what seemed like hours, Garfield accidentally flopped onto the basement stairs.

"Saved!" he cried.

He rocketed up the stairs. Hurling himself at the basement door, Garfield flattened it . . . and Jon, too!

"Garfield?" said Jon from under

the door. "Garfield, is that you? What's going on? What were you doing in the basement?"

"Breaking every bone in my body," Garfield wheezed as he lay panting on the kitchen floor.

"The light was out. I thought no one was down there," said Jon. "That's why I shut the door. By the way, the doorknob is stuck in my belly button."

"Big deal." Garfield shrugged. "A little operation and you'll be as good as new. In the meantime you should know that we have a very dangerous beast in our basement. We have to get out of here. I'll grab Odie, the mice, and my teddy bear. You grab the refrigerator and meet me at the car."

"Garfield—"

Garfield clamped his paw over Jon's mouth.

"No questions, Jon. I'll explain everything when we reach our new home in Outer Siberia. Now let's go!"

"Garfield," Jon tried again, "you're acting very strangely, even for you. Did you fall on your head? Maybe I should take you to the vet."

But Garfield was too terrified to listen. He rushed into Jon's bedroom. Grabbing Odie and Herb firmly by their tails, he pulled them out from under the bed.

"We're leaving," said Garfield. "Follow me."

"Right, cat," Herb agreed. "I'm with you. No more basements. No more beasts. I say we head for Wisconsin. Cheese country. Acres of cheese, as far as the eye can see. By the way, cat—where's Zeke?"

Garfield halted in mid-step. "Zeke?"

"Zeke," Herb repeated. "Mousy guy, about my height. You remember."

"Oh no!" exclaimed Garfield, smacking his fist against his forehead. "Zeke must still be in the basement! He's trapped in the basement with the beast!"

Garfield roared back into the kitchen, followed by Odie and Herb. They stampeded right over Jon, who had just gotten to his feet.

"I think I'm going to have to put a

stoplight in here," Jon moaned.

The three animals braked at the top of the basement stairs. Garfield called out, "Zeke! Zeke! Can you hear me?"

At first there was no answer.

"Poor Zeke," sniffed Herb. "All he ever wanted was a decent meal. Instead, he became one."

Then they heard something. It seemed to come from far away. "Cat? Cat? Can you hear me?"

"Aaargh!" groaned Garfield. "Can you believe this? Now I have to go back down in the basement to rescue that mouse. A cat saving a mouse! If this ever gets out, I'll be kicked out of the felines' union."

He turned to Odie and Herb. "Listen up, slackers!" he commanded. "I may be crazy for going down there, but I'm not crazy enough to go down there alone. This time you're coming with me. And that's an order!"

The mouse and the pup snapped to attention and saluted.

Garfield yanked open a kitchen drawer. "Odie, take this," he said, handing a flashlight to the dog. He grabbed a rolling pin for himself.

"We take no prisoners," Garfield muttered. He raised the rolling pin high above his head. "Hang on, Zeke!" he shouted. "Help is on the way!"

Jon watched Garfield, Odie, and Herb disappear down the basement steps. He shook his head. "This may be my house," he said, "but I never know what's going on."

Garfield, Odie, and Herb charged down the basement stairs. Reaching the bottom, they stopped to look around.

"Keep an eye out for the beast," Garfield warned. "If we spot him, Odie, you lay down a few gallons of dog drool. That should gross him out long enough for us to escape."

"Ruff," replied Odie, wagging his tongue.

"Save the spit for the beast, Mr. Waterworks!" said Garfield, shielding himself from Odie's spray. "We've got to find Zeke and get out of here. Shine that light around the basement."

Odie cast the flashlight beam around the room. The basement was even messier than before. Christmas lights and ornaments lay broken on the floor. Shredded newspapers hung from the rafters. Junk that had been stored in boxes was scattered everywhere.

"Wow," said Herb. "You must have had some fight with the beast."

"I was lucky to get out alive," Garfield told him.

He cupped his paw around his mouth. "Mouse? Mouse?" he called softly.

"Zeke? Are you there?" whispered Herb.

"Over here," said Zeke.

"Over where?"

"In the toaster."

The three rescuers scrambled over

to the old toaster on Jon's workbench. They shined the light inside.

"Hey! Dim the spotlight, will you?" squeaked Zeke. "You're frying my eyeballs!"

"Sorry," said Garfield, pushing the flashlight farther away.

"What are you doing in there, Zeke?" Herb asked.

"I'm making toast," Zeke replied sarcastically. "I ducked in here when the cat went bananas. Otherwise, he'd have squashed me for sure."

"Well, you can come out now," said Garfield.

"I wish I could. But I'm stuck."

"I can fix that," Garfield assured him. "Everybody stand back."

The fat cat examined the toaster closely. "I'll just give it a little tap," he said. Then he whacked it hard with

the rolling pin. The toaster popped, shooting Zeke into the air. He landed softly in Garfield's open palm.

"Good job, cat," said Zeke.

"Easy as burned toast," Garfield replied. "Now let's get out of here. I don't like being beast-bait."

Just then, they heard the strange sound again. Instantly, the fur stood up on all four necks. "It's alive," croaked Garfield.

"It's where we heard it before," Zeke murmured. He pointed to the canvas-covered table.

Garfield gritted his teeth. "We have some unfinished beast business," he said. "And I think it's about time we finished it."

He led the group over to the table. "On the count of three, I'm going to pull back the canvas," he whispered. "Odie, you hit the beast with a drool barrage. I'll bash it with the rolling pin. Mice, you do whatever you can."

"We'll nibble its toes until it begs for mercy," hissed Zeke.

Garfield took hold of the canvas. "Ready?"

Odie and the mice held their breath. Garfield tightened his grip on the rolling pin.

"One . . . two . . . I hope this isn't a big mistake . . . three!"

Garfield threw back the canvas.

"ATTACK! . . . Huh?"

Garfield, Odie, and the mice gasped in surprise.

Eight frightened eyes stared into the beam of Odie's flashlight. Eight eyes peeking out from little black masks.

"Raccoons?" said Garfield.

"Please, don't hurt my children," the mother raccoon pleaded. She clasped her three cubs to her chest.

"Raccoons," Garfield repeated. He turned to the mice. "This is your beast?

A mother raccoon and three tiny cubs? I thought you said it was 'huge'?"

"It was dark," Zeke told him with a shrug. "I guess we never really got a good look at it."

"Everything looks huge to a mouse," Herb explained.

"And what's *your* excuse, cat?" Zeke demanded. "You thought it was a huge monster, too."

Garfield gave an embarrassed grin. "Yeah, well, everything's bigger when you're afraid of it."

Now that everyone was over the shock, it was time to hear the mother raccoon's story.

"We were living in the woods at the end of the block," she began. "Three days ago the bulldozers came. The cubs and I were asleep. The machines started ripping out all the trees. We had to run for it. But there was no place to go. There are no other woods close by. I just wanted a place where the cubs would be safe for a few days. When I saw the hole in your basement window, I thought it was our best chance."

Garfield and the others nodded in sympathy.

"Of course, it hasn't worked out all that well," the raccoon admitted.

"There's no food here. All I've been able to find is a little cheese. And there's so much noise in this basement, the cubs are scared to death."

"Sorry about that," said Garfield. "I'm afraid we all had a slight case of craziness."

"If you'd just let us stay here a few more days," the mother raccoon asked. "Just till I can find a new home. But I hate to go looking and leave the cubs alone in this creepy place."

Garfield looked around the dark and cluttered room. "I guess it isn't exactly a resort, is it?"

"That's right, Garfield," said Zeke. "This gloomy basement is no place for kids. It's really no place for anybody, except spiders."

Garfield rubbed his chins. "Maybe we can find them something better."

"But where?" asked Zeke. "Like she said, there are no woods around here."

"That's true," Garfield replied. "But there are better places to live."

Zeke looked into Garfield's eyes. Amazement spread over the mouse's face. "Cat, you don't mean . . ."

Garfield smiled.

Garfield slumped in the easy chair, his gaze fixed on the TV screen. A big bowl of buttered popcorn rested on his lap.

Zeke scampered across the carpet and up the side of the chair. He sat down on the arm beside the cat.

"How's it going?" asked Zeke.

"Good," said Garfield, stuffing popcorn in his mouth.

"Off the diet, I see." Zeke helped himself to a kernel of popcorn.

"Yeah. I've almost got my figure back," Garfield boasted. "Of course, if

Jon sees another mouse . . ." He glanced sideways at Zeke.

"Don't worry," Zeke assured him. "Herb and I are staying out of sight."

"So life under the kitchen sink is working out then?" Garfield asked.

"Just fine," Zeke replied. "It's nice and cozy. And Herb couldn't be happier. He's back there chewing on a sponge right now."

"Glad to hear it," said Garfield.

"So what's on the tube?" the mouse asked.

"It's a special called *Dogs Are Even Dumber Than You Thought*. Look, that dog is taking a bath."

"What's so dumb about that?" Zeke wondered.

"He's taking it in the toilet."

"I see what you mean. By the way, how have the *other* arrangements been working out?"

"So far, so good," said Garfield. "Of course, if Jon ever looks in the back of his closet . . ."

Suddenly they heard a startled cry.

Zeke dove under the sofa. Garfield began shoveling popcorn into his mouth as fast as he could.

Jon Arbuckle trudged into the room, a stunned expression on his face.

"Garfield, I was just looking in the back of my closet," he said. "You won't believe this, but I have baby raccoons in my jogging shorts."

"Look at it this way, Jon," Garfield replied cheerfully. "It's better than having a beast in the basement!"